THIS WALKER BOOK BELONGS TO:

For Laura and Harry and Tilly

M.W.

For Frances

T.M.

First published 1991
by Walker Books Ltd, 87 Vauxhall Walk
London SE11 5HJ

This edition published 1993

6 8 10 9 7 5

Printed in Spain

British Library Cataloguing in Publication Data
A catalogue record for this book is
is available from the British Library.
ISBN 0-7445-3018-0

THE TOYMAKER

a story in two parts

Written by

MARTIN WADDELL

Illustrated by

TERRY MILNE

WALKER BOOKS
AND SUBSIDIARIES
LONDON · BOSTON · SYDNEY

1 Once upon a time there was a toymaker called Matthew. He loved making toys. He worked hard all day long tap-tap-tapping and stitch-stitch-stitching. He sold the toys he made to people who came to his shop, so that he could make money to keep himself and his daughter, Mary.

Mary was not strong.
She could not go out to play with
the other children.
She stayed inside and watched
them through the shop window.
Sometimes she was lonely.

Matthew wanted to make her happy
so he made her special toys.
They were dolls.
He made them very carefully,
so that each doll looked like
one of the children who played
outside the shop window.

Mary played with the dolls.
She called them Max
and Lily and Bertie,
after the children outside.
They made her happy.
Because she was happy,
she grew stronger.
At last she was able to go
outside to play.

She played and she played
and she played.
The dolls sat in the shop
window, watching.
Matthew watched too,
as he worked.
He smiled when she laughed
because he loved her.

No one played with the dolls
any more.
Matthew thought that Mary
had forgotten them.
He put them safely on a shelf
at the back of the shop.

People saw the dolls and asked,
"How much is this one?"
But Matthew said,
"They are not for sale.
They belong to Mary."
He would not sell the dolls,
not a single one,
for they were his memories
and they kept him company.

 Once upon another time
an old lady came to the
toyshop with her grand-
daughter, Jane. The toyshop
was empty and deserted.
"I wanted you to see it just once before it
was sold," the old lady told Jane. "This was
your great granpa's shop, where I lived
when I was a little girl."

"Was he the one who made my
  Noah's Ark?" Jane asked.
"He made lots of toys,"
  the old lady said.
"Where are they?" Jane asked,
  looking round at the dusty shelves.
"They are all gone now!" said the
  old lady, and she sat still, gazing out
  through the window.

Jane went looking for toys,
just in case.
And she found some
in a dusty cupboard
at the back of the shop.

They were dolls.
She took them to the old lady,
because she didn't
want her granny to be sad,
and she thought the
dolls might make her smile again.

"Max and Lily and Bertie!"
the old lady said.
"They were my special toys.
I played with them here
when I was a little girl."
"Can I play with them?" Jane asked.
"I'm sure they would like that,"
the old lady said.
And Jane put the dolls in the
window of the shop, where they
could see the street outside.

An old couple passed
by the shop window.
The man stopped
and looked at the dolls.
"That's me, Lily!" he said.
"And that's me!" said his wife.
"And that's Bertie!"
They called to Bertie
to come and see.
"That's you, Bertie,"
the old man said.
"They are us,
the way we used to be."

The old people wanted
to buy the dolls and they came
into the shop and tried to persuade
the old lady to sell them.
But the old lady said,
"They are not for sale,"
and she would not sell them,
not a single one.

"But they are us!" Max said.
"You've got to sell them to us, Mary."
"I can't sell them to you,"
the old lady said.
"They belong to you already."
And she gave her old friends
the dolls that were themselves,
the way they used to be.

The old people were pleased,
but Jane wasn't.
All the dolls were gone
and she had none left to play with.
"I'll make you a doll,"
the old lady said.
"Just like the ones your
great granpa made for me!"

And she did.

She tap-tap-tapped and
stitch-stitch-stitched
very carefully
until the doll was made.

She made it with love,
for she had not forgotten.

MORE WALKER PAPERBACKS
For You to Enjoy

Also by Martin Waddell

CAN'T YOU SLEEP, LITTLE BEAR?
illustrated by Barbara Firth
Winner of the Smarties Book Prize and the Kate Greenaway Medal

"The most perfect children's book ever written or illustrated...
It evaporates and dispels all fear of the dark."
Molly Keane, The Sunday Times

0-7445-1316-2   £4.99

THE HIDDEN HOUSE
illustrated by Angela Barrett
Winner of the W H Smith Illustration Award

The classic tale of three wooden dolls and the
changing fortunes of the house in which they live.

"An atmospheric fable... The mystery in the text is
enhanced by fine, evocative illustrations." *The Independent*

0-7445-1797-4   £4.99

THE TOUGH PRINCESS
illustrated by Patrick Benson

"Breaks all the conventions of the traditional fairy tale... Spirited and energetic colour
pictures add further humour to this highly enjoyable story." *Child Education*

0-7445-1226-3   £4.50

Walker Paperbacks are available from most booksellers, or by post from B.B.C.S., P.O. Box 941, Hull, North Humberside HU1 3YQ
24 hour telephone credit card line 01482 224626

To order, send: Title, author, ISBN number and price for each book ordered, your full name and address,
cheque or postal order payable to BBCS for the total amount and allow the following for postage and packing:
UK and BFPO: £1.00 for the first book, and 50p for each additional book to a maximum of £3.50.
Overseas and Eire: £2.00 for the first book, £1.00 for the second and 50p for each additional book.
Prices and availability are subject to change without notice.